For the dearest moon babies in the whole universe: Elizabeth, Ryan, and Danny—K.J.

For Mema, my grammie—A.H.

G. P. Putnam's Sons
an imprint of Penguin Random House LLC, New York

G. P. Putnam's Sons is a registered trademark of Penguin Random House LLC.

Visit us online at penguinrandomhouse.com

Library of Congress Cataloging-in-Publication Data
Names: Jameson, Karen, author. | Hevron, Amy, illustrator.
Title: Moon babies / by Karen Jameson ; illustrated by Amy Hevron.
Description: New York, NY : G. P. Putnam's Sons, [2019]
Summary: Illustrations and rhyming text follow baby moons as they awaken in their crescent cradles, have an outing, storytime, and more, then get kisses from grammies as they return to sleep. Identifiers: LCCN 2017040535 | ISBN 9780525514817 (hc)
| ISBN 9780525514824 (epub fxl cpb) | ISBN 9780525514848 (kf8/kindle)
Subjects: | CYAC: Stories in rhyme. | Moon—Fiction. | Babies—Fiction. Classification:
LCC PZ8.3.J1486 Moo 2019 | DDC [E]—dc23
LC record available at https://lccn.loc.gov/2017040535

Manufactured in China by RR Donnelley Asia Printing Solutions Ltd.
ISBN 9780525514817
1 2 3 4 5 6 7 8 9 10

Design by Eileen Savage. Text set in Maiandra.
The art was done in acrylic and pencil on wood and digitally collaged.

moon babies

Karen Jameson

illustrated by Amy Hevron

putnam

G. P. PUTNAM'S SONS

In the starry dark of night,
a secret moon world comes to light.
Make a wish and you just might
visit baby moons tonight.

Crescent cradles hang in rows.
In each pod, a small orb glows.
Safe and snug. Nestled deep.
This is where the moon babes sleep.

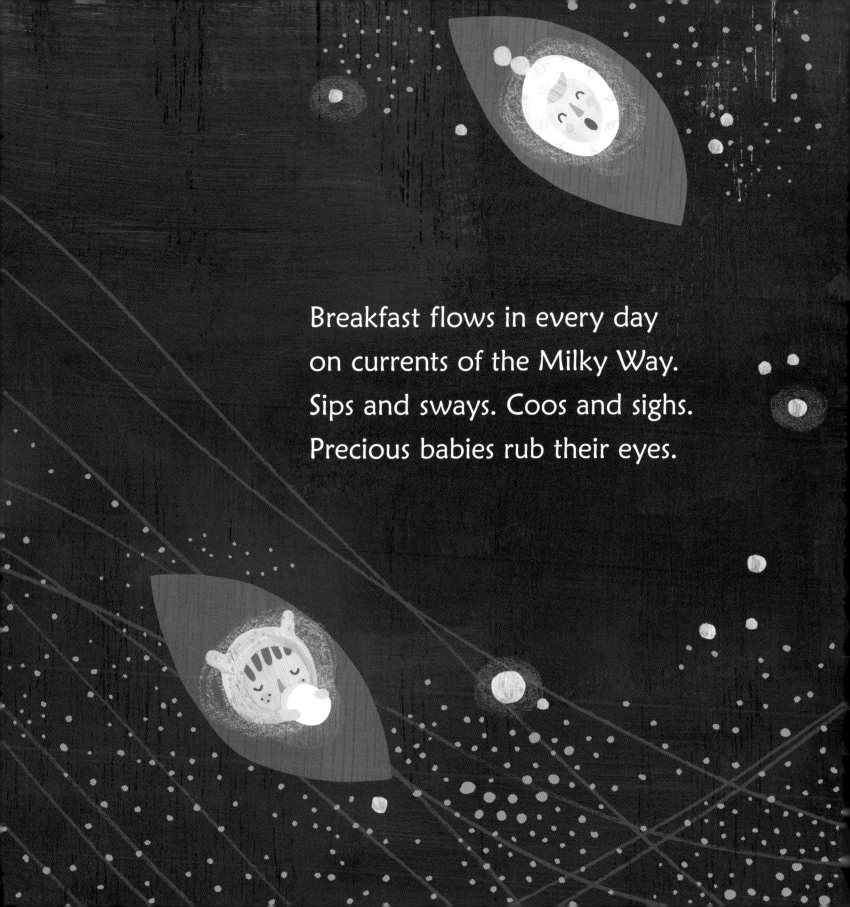

Breakfast flows in every day
on currents of the Milky Way.
Sips and sways. Coos and sighs.
Precious babies rub their eyes.

Up at moonrise. Lots to do.
Grammies dress our tiny crew.
Playtime outfits, hats and booties.
Off for moonwalks go these cuties.

Wobble-bobble, step and stumble.
Babies try but take a tumble.
Almost spinning. Startled, *PLOP!*
First time whirling like a top.

Morning outing. Starlight Park.
Toddlers swing and moon dogs bark.
Back and forth. To and fro.
Soaring high and dipping low.

The carousel's their favorite ride.
Round and round the kiddies glide.
Orbiting to merry tunes.
Fun and games for beaming moons.

Stacking moonstones—one, two, three.
Castle building. Watch and see.
Now the countdown—three, two, one.
Send them toppling just for fun!

Suppertime for every moon.
Little Dipper's turn to spoon.
Steamy porridge, smooth and white.
Come on, babies, one more bite!

Moonset's coming. Time to scrub
in a grand celestial tub.
Splashing play and bubble fun.
Stardust powder when they're done.

Snuggle up for nursery rhymes.
Treasured once-upon-a-times.
Mother Goose and dear Bo-Peep.
Babies nod off, counting sheep.

Little ones in softest jammies,
all tucked in by doting grammies.
Lullabies 'neath velvet skies.
Nighty-night, you moonie-pies!

Grammies kiss sweet tots by row,
whisper that they love them so.
Cradles sway from side to side.
Babies drift off, rock-a-byed.

In the starry dark of night,
a secret moon world dims its light.
Close your eyes and you just might
dream of baby moons tonight.